One bright, sunny morning in a corner of an old farmyard, a mother duck watched proudly as her ducklings hatched from their eggs. The five new ducklings were tiny and covered with soft, yellow feathers.

The Lovable
UGLY DUCKLING

Retold by **Kate Sullivan Watkins**

from a story by Hans Christian Andersen

Illustrated by **James Finch**

Art Directed by
Susie Garland

All art and editorial material is owned by Dalmatian Press.

ISBN: 1-57759-473-8

11217a/The Lovable Ugly Duckling

01 02 03 LBM 10 9 8 7 6 5 4 3 2 1

But the mother duck was puzzled because one egg did not hatch. This egg was much larger than the others were.

An old duck came waddling down the path and stopped to admire the new ducklings. "What's wrong with that egg?" the old duck asked. "I don't know," the mother replied, "but for some reason, it won't hatch." The old duck looked carefully at the egg. "Well, that's a turkey egg," she said. "Leave it alone and go teach your new babies how to swim."

"No," said the mother duck. "I've taken care of this egg for this long. I will stay with it until the duckling hatches."

The mother duck continued to sit until the large egg began to wobble and crack. Finally, out came an unusual looking baby bird. He was covered with rough, gray feathers, and he was much bigger than the other ducklings. His feet were large and clumsy, and his neck was long and skinny.

When the other birds in the farmyard saw him, they began to squawk. "What an ugly duckling!" honked the geese. "A very strange duckling indeed!" clucked the hens. Even the turkeys laughed at the way the new baby looked.

The poor baby duckling really did feel ugly. He made his way to a nearby lake to hide in the tall grass. He stayed hidden all summer long.

One night when the moon was shining brightly on the lake, the lonely duckling saw winged creatures gliding through the sky. Three magnificent swans cast graceful shadows as they flew through the night. The duckling stood still to admire them. Oh, how he longed to fly.

When winter came to the lake, the duckling grew cold and he had trouble finding food to eat. One morning, the duckling slipped on the ice of the frozen lake. A kind farmer found him lying helpless and scared on the ice. The farmer wrapped him in his coat and carried him back to the nice, warm barn. The duckling stayed in the barn, and the farmer took care of him for the rest of the long, harsh winter.

Spring finally arrived, and the farmer led the duckling out of the barn. The duckling had grown, and felt stronger than ever before. He flapped his wings gently in the warm light of the sun. To his surprise, he flew right off the ground into the bright sky.

He landed near some reeds at the edge of a peaceful pond. He could hear children playing nearby on the bank, and once again, he saw the lovely swans. This time they were drifting through the water.

Afraid that they might laugh at him, the ugly duckling lowered his head in shame. As he looked down at the reflection in the still water, he saw another swan that was just as splendid as the others.

After a moment, he realized he was staring at his own reflection. He was amazed at how beautiful he had become. He was not an duckling! In fact, he never was a duckling at all, but a swan in the making. He glided into the water and joined the other swans. When the children saw him, they began to shout. "Look at the new swan. He is the most splendid of them all!"

He was no
longer an ugly
duckling, but a
graceful and
beautiful swan.
With this
proud thought,
his heart
almost burst
with happiness
and joy.